A NOTE TO PARENTS

When your children are ready to "step into reading," giving them the right books—and lots of them—is as crucial as giving them the right food to eat. **Step into Reading Books** present exciting stories and information reinforced with lively, colorful illustrations that make learning to read fun, satisfying, and worthwhile. They are priced so that acquiring an entire library of them is affordable. And they are beginning readers with an important difference—they're written on four levels.

Step 1 Books, with their very large type and extremely simple vocabulary, have been created for the very youngest readers. **Step 2 Books** are both longer and slightly more difficult. **Step 3 Books,** written to mid-second-grade reading levels, are for the child who has acquired even greater reading skills. **Step 4 Books** offer exciting nonfiction for the increasingly proficient reader.

D1534195

Library of Congress Cataloging-in-Publication Data:
O'Connor, Jane. Molly the brave and me. (Step into reading. A Step 2 book) SUMMARY: Beth
admires her friend Molly's courage, but on a visit to Molly's country home, Beth surprises
herself with her own bravery when the two become lost within the maze of a cornfield.
ISBN: 0-394-84175-1 (pbk.); 0-394-94175-6 (lib. bdg.) [1. Courage–Fiction. 2. Friendship–Fiction.
3. Country life–Fiction] I. Hamanaka, Sheila, ill. II. Title. III. Series.
PZ7.0222Mo 1990 [E] 89-10864

Manufactured in the United States of America   1 2 3 4 5 6 7 8 9 0

STEP INTO READING is a trademark of Random House, Inc.

Step into Reading

MOLLY the BRAVE and ME

By Jane O'Connor
Illustrated by Sheila Hamanaka

A Step 2 Book

Random House New York

Molly has guts.

She has more guts than anybody

in the second grade.

She can stand at the top

of the monkey bars

on one foot.

She doesn't mind it
when Nicky hides dead water bugs
in her desk.

And if big kids pick on her,

Molly tells them to get lost.

Molly is so brave.

I wish I was like her.

Today on the lunch line

Molly said to me,

"Beth, can you come to our house

in the country this weekend?

It is lots of fun there."

Wow!

I guess Molly really likes me.

That made me feel good.

But I have never been away from home.

What if I get homesick?

What if they eat stuff I don't like?

What if there are lots

of wild animals?

I was not sure I wanted to go.

I sat at a table with Molly.

I said,

"Gee, Molly. It sounds neat.

Only I don't know

if my parents will say yes."

That night

Molly's mom called my mom.

My mom said yes.

So how could I say no?

It was all set.

Molly's parents were going

to pick me up on Saturday morning.

Friday night I packed my stuff.

Later my mom tucked me in bed.

"I'm scared I'll miss you," I said.

"I bet I'll cry all the time.

Then Molly will think

I'm a big baby.

And she won't like me anymore."

My mom hugged me.

"You will have fun.

And Molly will understand

if you are a little homesick."

Then my mom kissed me two times.

"One kiss is for tonight.

The other is for tomorrow night

when you will be at Molly's house."

Molly's parents came early

the next morning.

I was scared,

but I was excited, too.

Most of all

I did not want to look

like a wimp around Molly.

So I waved good-bye to my parents

and hopped in the back seat.

Molly's dog sat between us.

"This is Butch," said Molly.

Right away Butch started licking me.

I'm kind of scared of big dogs.

But did I show it?

No way!

I acted like I loved

getting dog spit all over my face!

By noon we got to Molly's house.

It sat all alone

at the top of a hill.

"This was once a farm,"

Molly's mom told me.

"It's 150 years old."

I like new houses.

They haven't had time

to get any ghosts.

But I didn't say that

to Molly's mom.

Right after lunch

we went berry picking.

That sounded like fun.

Then I saw all the beetles

on the bushes.

I did not want to touch them.

But Molly just swatted them away.

So I gave it a try too.

"Hey! this is fun," I said.

"I have never picked food before."

We ate lots and lots of berries.

Red juice got all over

my face and hands.

I pretended it was blood

and I was a vampire.

I chased Molly all around.

"You know what?" I told her.

"I am really glad that

   I came to your house."

Later we went looking for wild flowers.

That sounded nice and safe to me.

We walked all the way down to a stream.

A big log lay across the stream.

Molly ran right across it.

Boy, what guts!

Butch ran across too.

I stared at the log.

"Aren't there any wild flowers

on this side?" I asked.

Molly shook her head.

"The best ones are over here.

Come on, Beth. Don't be scared.

Just walk across—

it's easy."

"Okay," I told myself.

"Quit acting like a wimp."

I started taking tiny steps
across the log.

Near the end I slipped.

Oof! Down I went.

"Are you all right?" Molly asked.

I nodded,

but my backside really hurt.

We picked flowers for a while.

And when we left,

I crawled across the log.

Molly didn't tease me.

Still I knew I looked like a jerk.

On the way back to the house

Butch saw a rabbit

and chased it into a field of corn.

"Dumb dog!" said Molly.

"He will never catch that rabbit.

We'd better go and find him."

"Oh, rats!" I thought,

but I went in after Molly.

We followed the sound

of Butch's barks.

Boy, was that field big!

The corn was way over our heads,

and it seemed to go on for miles.

At last we spotted Butch.

Molly ran and hugged him.

Then she pulled me by the arm.

"This place is creepy,"

Molly said.

"Let's get out of here."

That was fine with me!

But it was not so easy getting out.

All the corn looked the same.

It was hot and hard to see.

Bugs kept flying in our faces.

It felt like we were walking

around and around in circles.

"Can't Butch help us find the way?"

I asked.

Molly shook her head.

"Butch can't find his own doghouse."

Then Molly started blinking hard.

And her nose got all runny.

"Beth," she said.

"We're really stuck in here.

I'm scared."

Molly scared?

I could not believe it!

I held her hand.

"Don't be scared," I told her,

even though I was scared too.

"We'll get out of here."

Then I got an idea.

"Come on," I told Molly.

I started to walk down the space

between two rows of corn.

I did not make any turns.

I stayed in a straight line.

"Pretend this is a long street,"

I said.

"Sooner or later

we have to come to the end of it."

And at last we did!

Molly and I hugged each other

and jumped up and down.

Woof! Woof! went Butch.

"Hot stuff!" said Molly.

"You got us out."

When we got back to Molly's house,

her mother said,

"Where have you girls been?

It is almost time for dinner."

Molly told her parents

about following Butch into the corn.

Then she put her arm around me.

"I was scared stiff,"

Molly told them.

"But Beth wasn't scared at all.

Boy, does she have guts!"

Guts? Me?

I couldn't believe my ears!

Dinner was great.

We cooked hot dogs on sticks over a fire.

And there was plenty of corn

on the cob.

"Oh, no! Not corn!"

Molly and I shouted together.

But we each ate three ears anyway.

Right before bed

I did get a little homesick.

Molly's mom gave me a big hug.

That helped.

Then Molly told me

I was her best friend.

We locked pinkies on it.

That helped too.

Maybe Molly was right.

Maybe I really am

a kid with guts!